This book belongs to:

_____

My first day of school:

_____

Don't
Go to
School!

Don't Go to School!

written by Máire Zepf

illustrated by Tarsila Krüse

STERLING CHILDREN'S BOOKS

New York

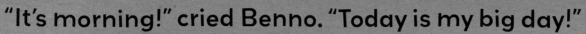

"It's morning!" cried Benno. "Today is my big day!"

Benno got dressed in his brand-new school outfit.
He looked terrific.

"Mommy!" he called. "Get up!
I can't be late for school on my very first day!"

Next it was time for a hearty breakfast.
"Now I'm ready," he said.

He put on his brand-new coat.
He was REALLY excited!
He only had one problem.

It was Mommy.

"Don't go to school!" she wailed.

"Stay here with me, Benno!"

Benno spoke to her softly.
"New things are a little scary sometimes,
Mommy. But you'll be fine when you're there.
Wait and see."

Benno gave Mommy a warm hug and off they went to school, hand in hand.

Mommy looked around the playground.
"Let's go home, Benno," she said. "I don't know anyone here!"

"Don't worry, Mommy," said Benno. "You'll get to know the other parents in no time. They seem really nice!"

"Good morning!" said the teacher. "I'm Mrs. Nolan."

"Welcome! Come inside and see the classroom.
Don't be shy—we're all friendly here!"

Before long, Mommy was as happy as could be. She really enjoyed the sandbox.

And the kitchen corner was even more fun!

"Painting!" she cried. "I love painting!"

"Mommy, you are too big for school," Benno told her.
"You have to go home now."

"I don't want to go home!" cried Mommy.
"I like it here! And I want to stay at school with you!"

Benno had an idea. He kissed his own hands and filled Mommy's pocket with the kisses. "If you miss me during the day, put your hand in your pocket and pull out a kiss. Then you'll feel my love for you, even when we aren't together."

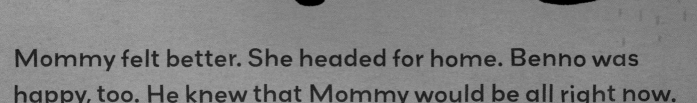

Mommy felt better. She headed for home. Benno was
happy, too. He knew that Mommy would be all right now.

"Time to dance!"
said the teacher.

"I love school!" Benno laughed.
He played and played with his new friends.

He drew pictures with colored pencils . . .

. . . and listened to the stories Mrs. Nolan read out loud.

What a surprise when Benno heard
the *ding a ling a ling* of the bell.
It was time to go home already!

Outside, Mommy was waiting for Benno.
Benno gave her a huge hug.
"You were so brave, Mommy!"

"Everything will be easier for you tomorrow—
just wait and see," said Benno.

To Lorcán, Cillian, and Áine—three stars who went to school very happily. —M. Z.

To Eric and Otto, who both made me Mom. —T. K.

STERLING CHILDREN'S BOOKS
New York

An Imprint of Sterling Publishing Co., Inc.
1166 Avenue of the Americas
New York, NY 10036

STERLING CHILDREN'S BOOKS and the distinctive Sterling Children's Books logo
are registered trademarks of Sterling Publishing Co., Inc.

Text © 2015 Máire Zepf
Illustrations © 2015 Tarsila Krüse

First published by Sterling Publishing Co., Inc. in 2017.
Published by arrangement with Futa Fata, An Spidéal, Galway, Ireland.

All rights reserved. No part of this publication may be reproduced, stored in a retrieval system,
or transmitted in any form or by any means (including electronic, mechanical, photocopying,
recording, or otherwise) without prior written permission from the publisher.

ISBN 978-1-4549-2359-6

Distributed in Canada by Sterling Publishing Co., Inc.
c/o Canadian Manda Group, 664 Annette Street
Toronto, Ontario M6S 2C8, Canada

For information about custom editions, special sales, and premium and corporate purchases,
please contact Sterling Special Sales at 800-805-5489 or specialsales@sterlingpublishing.com.

Manufactured in China

Lot #:

2 4 6 8 10 9 7 5 3

03/18

sterlingpublishing.com

The artwork for this book was created using a mix of traditional and digital media.
It was sketched in pencil and rendered digitally and in paint.